For my wonderful mother,
with much love.

First published in hardback in 1999 and in paperback in 2000 by Macmillan Children's Books
a division of Macmillan Publishers Limited
25 Eccleston Place, London SW1W 9NF, and Basingstoke
Associated companies worldwide.

ISBN 0 333 73068 2 (HB)
ISBN 0 333 73069 0 (PB)

1 3 5 7 9 8 6 4 2

A CIP catalogue record for this book is available from the British Library
Printed in Belgium by Proost

# Jamie
## and
# Vincent

by Pantelis Georgiou

Macmillan Children's Books

Jamie woke up early. He was staying at
Grandad's house while his mum was away
for a couple of days. Jamie liked staying
at Grandad's but he missed his mum.

Grandad had a new pet – a cat called Vincent.
Every morning Vincent would play in the garden
and try to catch butterflies, but he never could.

Jamie's mum didn't like cats because they made her
sneeze, so Jamie decided he didn't like cats, either.

"Why don't you play with Vincent?" said Grandad,
but Jamie never would.

"Grandad?" said Jamie.
"Mum said cats scratch.
Does Vincent scratch?"
    Grandad chuckled.
"No, Vincent doesn't
scratch," he replied.

After lunch Jamie hurried outside,
but he couldn't find Vincent anywhere.
  "He's sleeping over there," Grandad said,
pointing to the flowerbed.

Jamie stroked Vincent carefully.
"His fur is so soft, Grandad."
Grandad smiled.

"Grandad?" said Jamie. "Mum said that cats smell.
Does Vincent smell?"

"No, Vincent doesn't smell," Grandad replied.

Jamie sniffed Vincent. "He smells of *flowers*!" he said.
Grandad laughed.

In the afternoon it rained.

Vincent rushed inside and Jamie helped
dry him with a cloth. Vincent purred.

"He makes a loud noise, doesn't he?" said Jamie.

When it stopped raining, Jamie helped Grandad
pick vegetables from the garden for tea.

"Grandad?" said Jamie. "Mum said cats have got fleas.
Has Vincent got fleas?"

"No, Vincent hasn't got fleas," Grandad replied.

At tea-time Grandad poured Jamie a glass of milk.

"I don't like milk," said Jamie.

"Vincent likes milk," Grandad replied.

Jamie drank all his milk.

"That was nice, Grandad."

Grandad smiled.

In the evening Vincent sat on Grandad's lap.

"Grandad?" said Jamie.

"Mum said that cats ruin the furniture.
Does Vincent ruin the furniture?"

"No, Vincent doesn't ruin the furniture,"
replied Grandad.

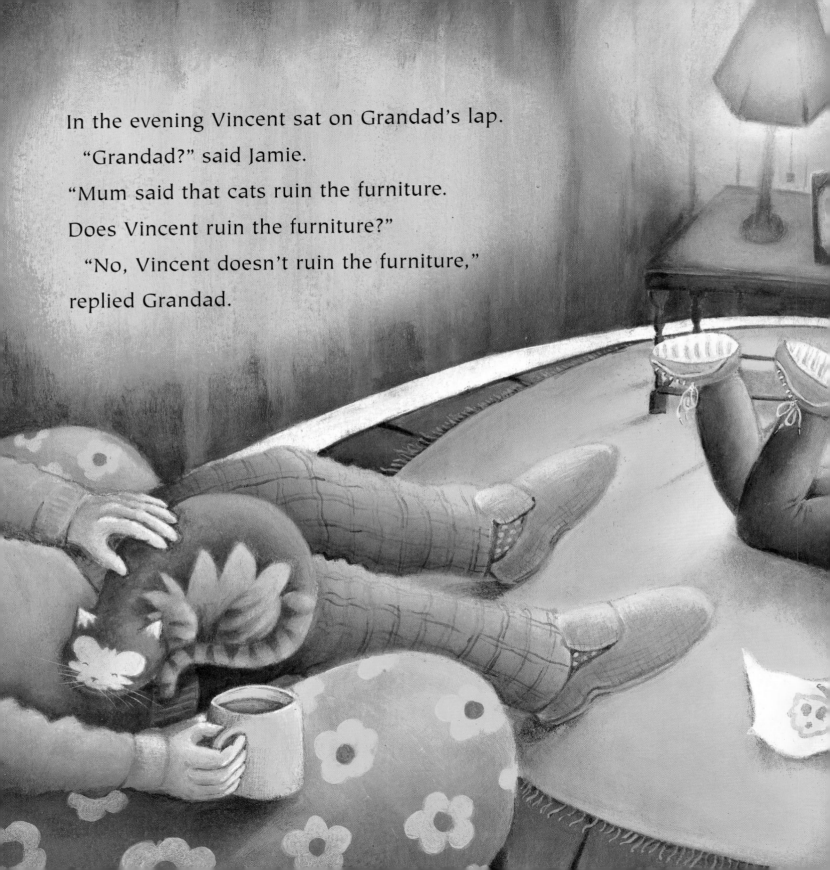

Jamie brushed his teeth before going to bed.

"See, Vincent likes to be clean, too!" Grandad said.

Jamie smiled. Vincent purred as he licked his fur.

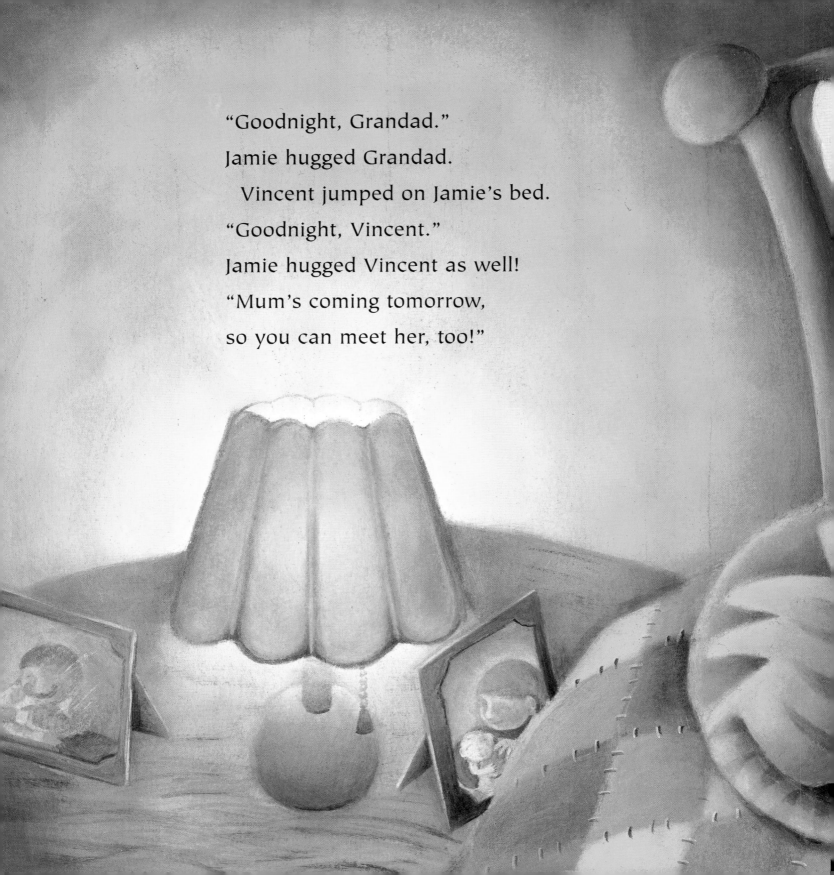

"Goodnight, Grandad."
Jamie hugged Grandad.
  Vincent jumped on Jamie's bed.
"Goodnight, Vincent."
Jamie hugged Vincent as well!
"Mum's coming tomorrow,
so you can meet her, too!"

The next day Jamie's mum came to collect him.

"Come and stroke Vincent, Mum," said Jamie.

Mum was worried that Vincent would make
her sneeze, but she stroked him carefully.

"Can we take him home with us?" asked Jamie.

Grandad smiled. "I think I might miss him, Jamie!
But he'll be here every time you come to stay."

"Can I come again soon?" asked Jamie.

"Of course you can," said Grandad.

And Vincent purred.